AF261250

www.summitwide.com

Printed via Amazon CreateSpace.

First Edition, December 2015

1 5 1 9 7 9 5 9 6 3

Where's the Popcorn / by Donald R. New ; illustrated by Brittney Moore.--First Edition

Summary: A story that follows the journey of one boy as he searches for popcorn.

ISBN: 978-1-5197-9590-0
[1. Boys-Fiction. 2. Popcorn-Fiction. 3. Travel-Fiction.]

Visit www.summitwide.com or www.donaldnew.com

DEDICATION:

This book is dedicated first and foremost to my wonderful children. Benjamin and Amelia, you two are the sparkles in my eyes. To my wife, you are my greatest inspiration. And finally, to all the parents out there who attempt to read this to their children. I hope you win the battle to keep them still long enough that you might read at least one more page.

Where's the Popcorn?

By: D. R. New

Illustrated by: Brittney Moore

I went on a trip,
I did, I did...

to find me some
popcorn
because I am a
kid.

I went to the
store
to look
around...

but there
was no
popcorn to be
found.

POPCORN
SALE

PUBLIC
LIBRARY

I went to the
library to
take a look...

but all I saw
were a bunch
of books.

POLICE

I went to the

police station

to file a

report...

but all the
cops were
late for
court.

POPCORN

I Went to the movies to explore...

but all I
found were
crumbs on
the floor.

I went to the farm to scout it out.

There Must
have been a
popcorn
drought.

I searched...

HIGH.

I searched...

low.

There was
no popcorn,
no matter
where I
would go.

So, I went home to observe...

A bowl of
popcorn,
ready to
serve!

I went on a trip, I did, I did...

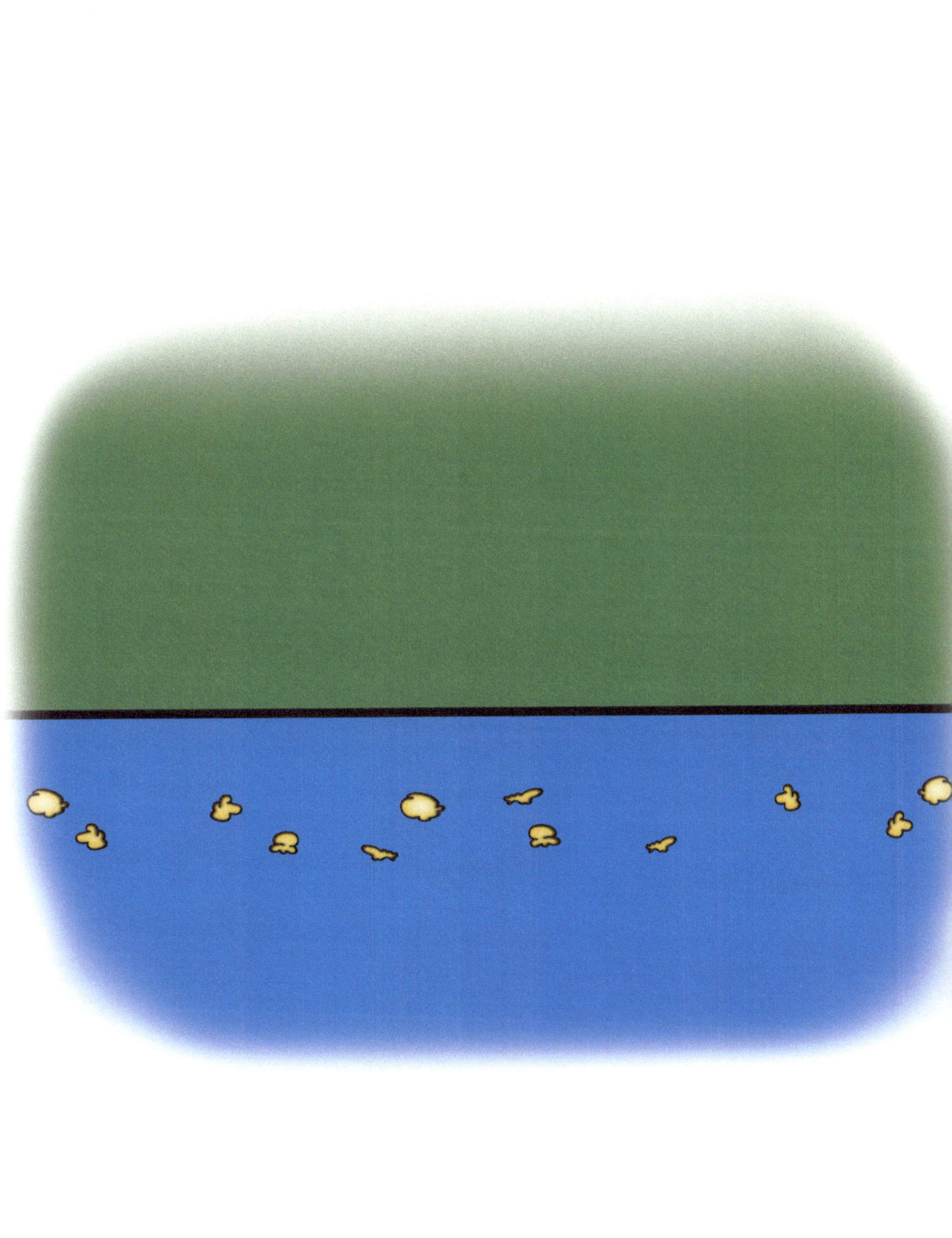

and found
some popcorn.
because I am
a kid.

THE

END.